"A beautiful, haunting meditation on love, fate, and the right to choose (if only the method of one's own destruction)."

— *CRIME READS*

"*Of Beasts* is a revelry of perversions, a bacchanalia of grotesquerie, a sermon of restless spirits wandering in the distant regions of the human and the inhuman, of the sacred and the utterly blasphemous. This is the kind of feverishly surreal and disquieting horror fiction that I adore."

— ERIC LAROCCA, AUTHOR OF
*THINGS HAVE GOTTEN WORSE
SINCE WE LAST SPOKE*

"*Of Beasts* is a dark, dreamlike hymn of love and devotion, made sharper by the blood and bruises. Best swallowed in one sitting."

— **ANDREW JOSEPH WHITE,**
AUTHOR OF *YOU WERENʼT*
MEANT TO BE HUMAN

OF BEASTS

HORROR

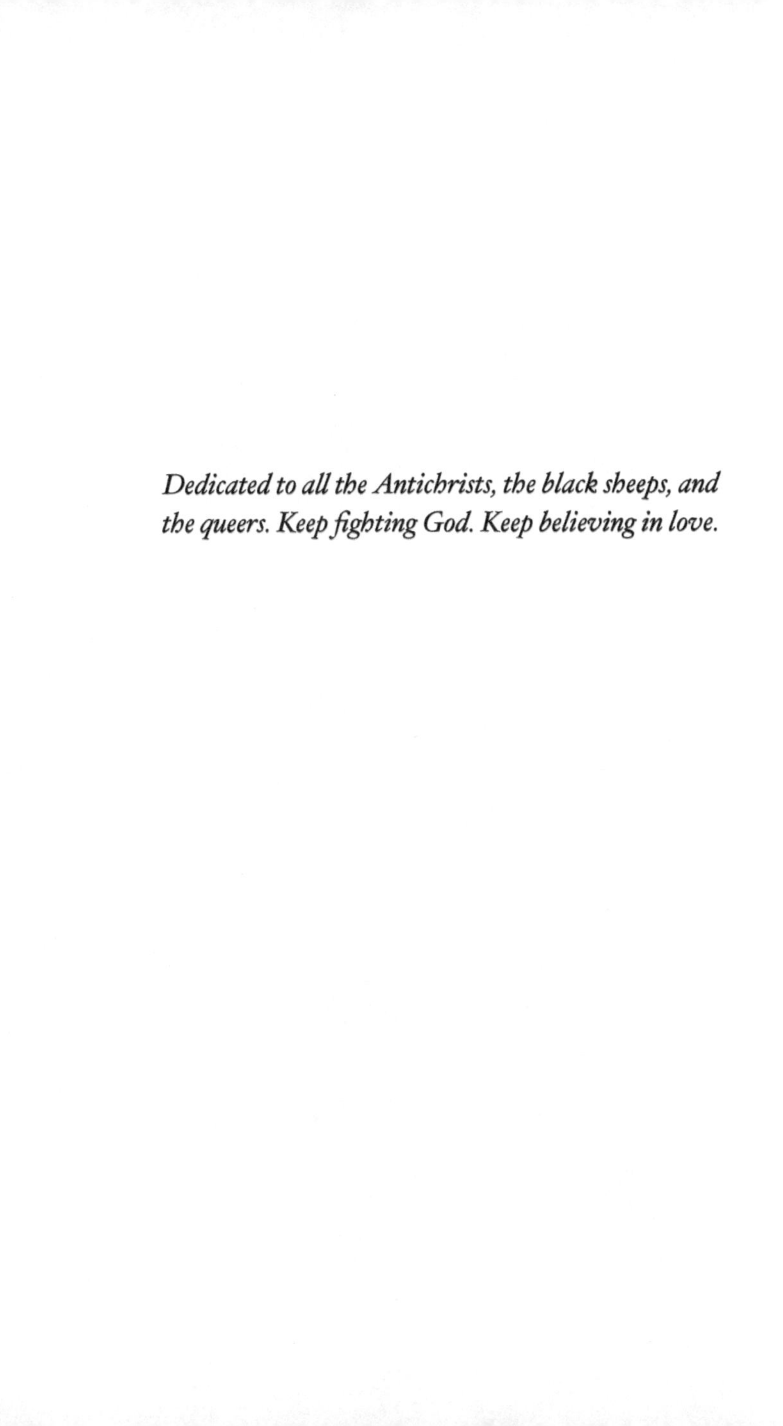

Dedicated to all the Antichrists, the black sheeps, and the queers. Keep fighting God. Keep believing in love.

OF BEASTS

M. JANE WORMA

DANTE WAS FUCKING THE LOCAL PASTOR.

Jude's sermon for the morning spoke of union and fruit to bear. "Man will not lie with man as he would woman," he read from the old pages. "Hedonistic," Jude had said. It was night and Dante was thinking of that sermon as he inched Jude's cock down his throat, thick enough to hurt, familiar enough to not.

He remembered when Jude was still in the pews with him. A roguish teenager that reminded him of gold, tanned skin from days spent under the sun, blond hair all the more rich against it, dark brown eyes like rye whiskey. That was before he would go off to ministerial training and come back as their new pastor, taking over for his retiring father who was growing too sick to manage it anymore. It was only a few years, but Jude returned taller. The muscle of him had slimmed in the time away from roaming around their small town, growing soft from days spent studying over scripture instead. Still, he had grown despite it. He was paler now, his hair and eyes more ghostly in that new skin.

Jude was no longer just a teenager. By the time he returned to take over the church from his father, he was already twenty-three. It hadn't even been a full four years, but could have been centuries with how much had eroded and reformed between them.

Back then, when they were both young, Jude had hardly ever given a glance to him. Dante was only a kid then, a fourteen-year-old brat. Jude hardly knew he existed.

Now, Jude couldn't stop staring at him.

Jude came into Dante's mouth without warning. With a sense of grace, Dante swallowed down the warmth pooling in the back of his throat, shuddering.

A hand was coiled tight in his shiny, soft black hair. Jude was keeping Dante there, down on his knees, refusing to let him pull back until he was finished. His scalp seared. Dante whined. Jude's grip tightened.

Dante didn't think Jude was cruel when he first tried to seduce him. But it was there, some raw primal need to wring out blood, cries, submission. It was biblical in a way, Dante thought. Being with Jude was like being stoned, an onslaught of abuse that left him bruised and bleeding. The way Jude held his wrists and ankles at times, his grip tightening more and more before a sudden release, felt like he wanted them to snap.

Though Jude never said it, Dante suspected he was the only one Jude was ever like this with. Tiffany, Jude's ex who he had dated for years before he went to ministry school, still lingered at the doorway after church to talk to him, laughing at anything he said and leaning in. Trish, another ex, brought him homemade baked sweets every other Sunday.

Dante noticed they never flinched. They always met Jude's eyes. It was hard to imagine they had ever been held down until they were begging, like Dante had.

Maybe it was because he was a boy. Maybe because he was already a secret. More likely, Dante suspected, because Dante was the only one Jude didn't try to keep face with. There was no image he was selling.

Jude could be anything he wanted with him.

His hair was released, Jude's hand now running through it, pushing his bangs back tenderly. Dante inched Jude's cock out of his mouth, pulling away with a wince. The back of his throat throbbed. Spit ran down his chin. In front of Dante was Jude's limp cock, still red, shiny in his own spit.

Jude reached down to curl his arms under Dante's and pulled him to his feet, holding him to his chest to lean on. Jude tucked himself back in his pants before running his hands through

Dante's hair again, slow, gentle. "You okay?" He asked.

Dante closed his eyes and nodded. Jude let him catch his breath, smoothing his hair. The spots where Jude had yanked the roots ached at the motion. Jude held him steady but his own breath was shaky as he settled down.

"Where does your mother think you are?" Jude asked.

"Tom's place."

"So you can stay," Jude said, and his arms encircled Dante completely and hauled him up like he was nothing. Dante was not small exactly, but he was slim and delicate. In Jude's hands, he might as well have been weightless.

Jude threw him down onto the bed, making Dante bounce from the force of it. He scoffed like he was offended, before laying down on his back, waiting as Jude crept over him.

It wouldn't be the first time Dante had stayed overnight. If anything, he was losing count. It was nearly a ritual at this point.

He told his mother he was staying at a friend's place. Jude lived alone. It was all too easy.

Dante could not explain the transition from budding crush to teeth-gritting, coveting need for Jude, but it happened. When Jude returned, paler, older, more solemn but voice exactly as soft and lulling as before, Dante wanted him like a dog wanted bleeding meat.

Would you just fucking look at me, Dante thought those first few weeks Jude had returned. *Just fucking look.* Sunday after Sunday, glazing over sermons and prayers in favor of that one obsessive thought running through his head. *Look at me.*

And then Jude did.

Dante couldn't remember who started it. One day they were alone in Jude's office, after hours. Dante said he was looking for guidance. He remembered wanting Jude in that moment. Wanted Jude to touch him. Wanted to touch

Jude. Then Jude and him were both on their feet, Dante held against the cool plaster wall while Jude crushed his mouth against his, the heady smell of Jude's cologne and sweat overwhelming him. Did he move towards Jude? Did Jude move towards him? It was as if any thought he had, Jude followed suit, to the point the lines blurred between the actual man and Dante's own fantasies.

Dante yielded under Jude's hands. He had no resistance as Jude slowly stripped him. No resistance as Jude held him down in bed, let his legs be pliant as Jude jerked them over his shoulders.

Dante was not the first guy Jude was attracted to. Regardless of what Jude said at the pulpit, what the town and other pastors said, what translations said, he would lay with as many men as he wanted.

It was a sin that never mattered much to him, and it was between him and God in the end. *Look the other way if you don't like it*, he muttered at his bible. But in all his days at the church and the ministries, through all his prayers and studies, he never got the sense God cared much either way.

So he had who he could.

There was his roommate from his missionary trip who made a point to not look away when the both of them changed. They ended up making out in Jude's bottom bunk late at night when everyone else was asleep, the dark keeping them safe and sound from anyone's discovery. Then there was the friend from his old high school, the one who was on the football team with him. They ended up jacking each other off in the locker room after practice one evening, when the rest of the team was long gone. Even when he went off to ministry school, he had managed to find another student who ended up in his room after a long night at the local bar.

The attraction was nothing new. Dante was simply the first one he maintained some semblance of a relationship with.

He was also the first one that wasn't his own age. Jude didn't want to like him. Before Jude went off to ministry, he had hardly even noticed who Dante was. Just a scrawny kid he saw every now and again in church, not anything he had the capacity to want.

The Dante that he came home to after all those years was such a different creature that it was startling whenever Jude did remember what he used to be.

He had turned beautiful. Smooth skin. Dark and rich black hair curling around his face, long enough for Jude to wrap his fingers in. A seductive gaze that Jude could not resist meeting, even as he preached, even as bible study met and the room was full of other teenagers and Jude shouldn't be thinking about those things at all, how it would feel to let him indulge in whatever it was Dante was yearning for in that look. But he did, again and again, the thoughts coiling around his head in gentle heat until it finally happened.

That first night in his office, he struggled to understand how his thoughts had crossed from his head and into the world, surprised when he realized Dante's body under his hands was actually corporeal and not a dream. *This can't be happening,* Jude thought as he leaned over Dante and crushed his mouth against his, Dante's fingers twisting into the collar of his shirt. *I didn't want this to happen.* But it did. And then it happened again, and again.

In the end, he had become a cliché.

Jude's hands wrapped around Dante's throat as they came close. It was an easy grasp, a slight pressure at the sides of his neck. Dante's eyes fluttered and his head went limp in Jude's hands, his breath hitching shallower. Jude picked up his pace, squeezed a little harder. Dante looked up at him with those bright brown eyes, so light and warm it was like a soft red had been pooled into them. Cinnamon, Jude thought. Earthly and stinging. Too beautiful to stand.

Jude wanted to destroy him at times. For a

moment, he could only think about crushing harder, the sensation of cartilage collapsing under his hands and the panicked white of Dante's eyes. His grip tightened. A small pulse fluttered against his palms.

"Jude," Dante choked out barely, a frightened wheeze in the sound. Still, that grip held him. Dante hit him with a fist. Nothing. His face was turning red, his chest tight. "Jude!" He hit him again hard enough to hurt his own fist against the bone of the man's shoulder.

Jude withdrew his hands suddenly like Dante's throat burned him. Dante took in a large, ragged breath before suddenly coughing hard. "Shit," Jude said. It wasn't the first time that had happened.

"Too much," Dante said. His chest heaved in frantic breaths, gasping so deep that Jude could see the wide expansion of his chest.

"I'm sorry," Jude said, voice thick and solemn. He reached out and ran his hand through Dante's hair, tucked it behind his ears. Gingerly he touched Dante's throat, fingertips barely there. The skin was pink. He hoped it would not bruise. The thought of Dante's neck wrapped in the dark purple shape of his own large hands made Jude shiver, although he could not say why exactly beyond the fear of being discovered.

"It's okay," Dante rasped. He collapsed back into the sheets.

Tension sat in the air around them. Jude sat on the bed, saying nothing, only listening to the light wheezing of Dante fill the room.

Minutes passed. Dante waited for Jude's next move, to crawl back on him. The man remained still instead, stiff. He could have been a statue.

"Jude?" Dante finally called out. "Do you want to..."

"Let's go to bed," Jude said. He stood up and walked away to the dresser, grabbing sleep pants and throwing a large shirt to Dante before he disappeared into the bathroom. In the entire exchange, Jude never met Dante's eyes. They went to sleep in the dense silence that hummed between them.

THAT NIGHT, DANTE DREAMED OF A BLACK desert and a voice booming from the sky.

Dante, it said, loud enough he could feel the sound roll through him and into the ground. The voice was strange, absent of any vocal quality he had ever known. It wasn't deep, it wasn't rough or sweet, it wasn't feminine or masculine or anything he had heard from another person. Like the voice his thoughts formed, it was only neutral, maybe not even a voice at all. Still, he could hear it.

Go to Jerusalem and rebuild the temple, and sit on the throne of Solomon.

A cold sweat broke over his skin. His spine chilled. "Why?" He asked. The desert wind cut through, sand running over his skin, sharp and piercing.

Dante: Go to Jerusalem and rebuild the temple, and sit on the throne of Solomon.

"No," Dante said. He took a step back, except there was nowhere to go. It was all just desert, the flatline of the horizon, and the voice surrounding him like air.

Dante: Go to Jerusalem and rebuild the temple, and sit on the throne of Solomon.

Dante: Go to Jerusalem and rebuild the temple, and sit on the throne of Solomon.

Dante: Go to Jerusalem and rebuild the temple, and sit on the throne of Solomon.

Dante:

An anthem of horns rang out and swelled over, all around him, drowning out even the voice, blaring louder and louder until it was all Dante could hear and feel, until it slipped under his skull, shaking into the core of him—

Dante woke up gasping. The dream was gone. The sound had stopped, the air quiet and serene, still. Outside the window, birds sang. Jude lay next to him, still sleeping, the man's dense back turned to him. Gentle sunlight eased into the room in a soft gold haze, the air sweet.

Despite it, Dante's heart still raced frantically in his chest as if he were still in that dream, an uncomfortable adrenaline running through him. He sat up in bed and pulled his knees in to hold. His eyes were wet, swollen, his face tear-streaked.

The bed shifted. Jude rolled over, half-lidded eyes glancing at Dante in a lazy haze. "Morning," he muttered, the word faint, like he was half asleep. Dante said nothing, afraid of what his voice might sound like.

Eventually Jude pushed himself up from bed

to sit. His hand went to Dante's hair to run his hand through it, tender. "Woah," Jude said at Dante's face, the wet surface of his cheeks glimmering in the sunlight. "Hey, hey, what's wrong?" Jude wanted to wrap an arm around and pull him in, except in that moment a sickening thought dropped into him that he was the reason Dante was crying.

"Nothing," Dante said. He rubbed at his face furiously. "It was just a bad dream. That's all."

A strange relief settled into Jude. Still, he reached across to touch him. "M' sorry. You're fine now."

Dante nodded. His breath had finally returned to normal, his heartbeat slowing even as that awful choir of horns lingered in his head, ringing. Dante left the bed and headed for the bathroom to get ready for the morning.

When he was dressed, Dante walked into the kitchen to find Jude waiting there, resting against the counter. A pot of coffee had been brewed and warmed the room, the smell of it soothing. Jude handed Dante a mug, the milk and sugar already stirred in the way he knew Dante preferred. It was another piece of information he shouldn't know, gathered after too many mornings spent together like this.

"Thanks," Dante said meekly. He took a seat on one of the stools by the kitchen island and sipped, allowing the warmth of it to seep into his hands. His face looked better now, Jude noticed. Tears gone, eyes less puffy and red.

"I had a dream too," Jude said.

"Oh yeah?" Dante asked. "What was in yours?"

"You," Jude said. He regretted it almost as instantly as he said it. A tension settled over Dante, some unreadable expression coming over his face. Jude didn't even know why he admitted Dante was in it at all. He could have said anything.

"What about me?" Dante asked.

Jude shrugged. "Maybe it's guilt. Maybe I'm fucking up too much."

Dante's eyebrows furled, confused, upset. "What happened in the dream, Jude?"

"Not much," Jude said. "I just saw you and... fire."

A ring of fire. A voice Jude could not bring himself to mention, the things it said to him.

Dante's grip on his mug tightened.

"Do you want to talk about yours?" Jude asked.

"No."

Jude stayed quiet, allowing the nervous silence to sit in the room between them. He understood Dante's refusal. There was more than he wanted to share from that dream. The image of it lingered still in Jude's mind, perfectly clear, as if he were still there.

Dante in a ring of fire, and Jude stepping in. A voice singing to him. Then Dante's head in his hands, severed at the neck. His eyes still bright and alive, that cinnamon color almost red in the light of the flames.

When Jude dropped Dante off at the old dirt street down from his house, under the cover of trees that blocked off the eyes of the main road so no one would notice him slipping out of the pastor's car, the two had hardly said a thing at all.

DANTE'S MOTHER TOLD HIM STORIES ABOUT his dad.

Wonderful stories. She said his name was Adam and that they met when she was traveling through Europe, backpacking. They married, of course. "It only took two weeks."

He died before Dante was born. "He would have loved you," she would tell him. "He did love you." They had never been to his grave. His mother said he was buried in France, his home country, and promised that one day they would visit. One day, always a day far off into the future. He had heard her say that so many times that the day no longer felt like a point in time in which they would reach but an idea, intangible and ever-existing.

There were no pictures of him. "We only took a few," she explained. All on a corner store disposable camera. "We weren't together for long before he passed... I would have taken more if I had known." She would softly berate herself at times for it. The camera had been lost before they could take it in to be developed. "I thought he had it, he thought I had it. We might have left it at a hostel, or I lost it when I moved. I don't know. I should have gotten it developed as soon as it was full."

It would be a few years until Dante contemplated how someone could have a wedding and come back without anyone having captured and printed a single picture.

It was only last winter that Dante found out the reality of his father. He was at Tristian's house, a friend who went to the same high school, the same youth group at church. They had been curled in the living room couch late at night, the dark drawing them into a strange and floating state, peaceful. The high from the joint they had shared an hour earlier in the bathroom, the window open to wash away the smoke and smell into the cool dark air, still sat deep in them. If Mrs. Walker, Tristian's mom, knew what they had been up to, she said nothing about it as she brought them mugs of hot chocolate and meandered between the living room and kitchen, cleaning up from the day.

He and Tristian had been talking about graduation and what they would do after college and Tristian said he'd like to take a gap year traveling around Europe.

"Yeah," Dante said, wistful. "I want to go to France one day. But I'd take my mom."

"With your mom? Why?"

"Well, my dad's buried there, and she's always wanted to visit." It was a little strange to say, he realized. He rarely said anything about his father. No one really ever asked. Everyone in the small town already knew him as the kid with a single mom, no father around.

"Your dad?" Both of the boys looked up to see Tristian's mother looking at them from the kitchen archway. She had a towel in her hand, Dante assumed for drying dishes, but she held nothing else. "Dante, I didn't know your mother found your father. I'm so sorry."

"Oh, it's okay," Dante said. "He's been dead for a long time. Before I was born. I mean I guess losing her husband was rough, but she's adjusted."

Her thin eyebrows tensed together, mouth tight in thought. "Your mother never married."

"Oh, she was," Dante said. "Before she moved here with me."

A cool apprehension came across her, and she looked at him with a certain, strange pity.

"Dante," she said, speaking with a voice that was carefully even and low. "Your mother's lived here her whole life."

By the time the dreams started nearly a year later, he would have almost forgotten the conversation. He did not ask his mother about it, and did not feel the need to. Nothing had changed for him, really. The idea of his father was still an ever-present, soothing fantasy, kept nestled deep and safe in the depths of his mind.

THE DREAMS CAME EVERY NIGHT.

Dante was back in the desert, sun beating down in a stinging heat. The voice rang out to him each time, suffocating.

Dante: Go to Jerusalem and rebuild the temple, and sit on the throne of Solomon.

Again and again, the voice echoing out across the land. Sometimes he was in a black desert again, only a faint blue night allowing him to make out the hills in the distance, sand between his toes. Sometimes he was in a circle of fire, with nothing else in the room besides him and the voice.

The worst was the desert under the sun, when it was illuminated, and he could see. He was always sitting on a towering throne, in a temple, looking down at the expanse of the land that scorched in golden light. In those dreams, the people gathered in clusters so thick that there was no ground to see. No sand. Only the sight of flesh all around, packed tight. Piles of slaughtered bodies. Swarms of people thrashing in frenzied worship.

At the end of those dreams, the voice spoke

to him and the sky parted, and Dante watched above still from his perch as fire rained down onto the bodies below.

The nights were relentless. Dante went to school with swollen eyes. At church, it was only Jude's voice that kept him awake, his body slumped in the pew and eyes fluttering every few minutes in a bid to close and slip away.

Jude did not have dreams while Dante was away. For nights, he slept alone in bed with a quiet mind, waking up from a cool and black sleep. He rested deep and easy, fresh in the mornings. Whatever had happened the last time, he had forgotten it already. The memory of holding Dante's head lingered in the back of his brain like a fog, distant and unclear. It was only a nightmare, and it was over.

It wasn't until Dante was back in his bed, wrapped under his arms, that Jude dreamed again.

All around him was light. Bright fire, orange and red flames dancing, shadows flickering over him. The heat seemed like it should be burning, but it was only warm. If anything, it felt nice, like sinking into the unwinding heat of a bath after trudging through a deep and bitter winter day.

The calm only lasted until Jude realized he was not alone in the ring of fire. Off beside him, in the middle of it, stood Dante. Suddenly Jude remembered his last dream. "No," he hissed. He almost reached out, only pulling his hands back as he remembered how this ended—the severed head wet in his palms. "Dante—"

A voice boomed around him.

Jude, you will slay Dante, and the beast will rise, and you will carry him to Jerusalem, and he will sit on the throne of Solomon.

The sound jolted through him. Jude twisted around, searching, but there was no other figure. He looked back to Dante to see he had taken a step forward. His eyes were strange. Glassy in the firelight, unfocused. "No," Jude begged. "I don't want to."

Jude, you will slay Dante, and the beast will rise, and you will carry him to Jerusalem, and he will sit on the throne of Solomon.

The voice swarmed them all around, the air taut with it. A shaky breath escaped him. He looked down at his hands to see a blade in his fist, silver edge shimmering in the firelight. Dante stepped closer, his face leaning up to Jude's. Without thinking, Jude watched himself put the blade to Dante's throat.

Jude, you will slay Dante.

"I'm sorry," Jude choked out. Dante was unresponsive, hypnotized. Or maybe he was only patiently waiting. His eyes were large black pools, deep and wet, the light dancing over them. The rich cinnamon color of them was even stronger now, redder than they had been before, highlighted in the flames of the room. Jude let himself sink into that gaze as if it could suspend them both, as if it was something he could take and keep with him selfishly.

Jude, the voice rang out again, cutting down into him.

Slay Dante.

In the morning, the two of them woke to a wrongness in the room. A sick tension had settled in the air with them. The dreams lingered around, the images replaying in the back of their skulls. Neither questioned how they both avoided looking at each other.

They slipped from bed without saying a word, got dressed, brushed their teeth. In the kitchen the silence swelled into an oppressive force as Jude made coffee, Dante sitting at the kitchen island and waiting. His eyes were swollen and pink. A blood vessel had broken in the left one, the bottom corner of it a harsh red starburst that hurt with each movement.

Jude set the mug in front of Dante. The teen cupped it between his hands and sipped, letting the warmth of it seep into him. It was the closest he felt to relief in weeks, able to sit in the comfort of Jude's kitchen, lazily resting at the counter, the dreams over for now.

"Dante," Jude said softly, ached. His hand reached out, the tip of a single finger tracing under Dante's hurt eye. "You look terrible."

Dante scoffed. "That's rude. You didn't think

I looked too terrible last night." He studied Jude, taking in the sullen expression. His skin seemed dull somehow, and there was a quiet agony in Jude's face. "You don't seem so hot either."

Jude frowned, pulling his hand back. He picked up his own coffee and leaned up against his counter, drinking while he stared off at a sun bright window. It was a Saturday and service would not be until later in the day. Normally he would take advantage and fuck Dante again. Drag him to the bedroom, or just unravel him on the island, the floor. The days and weeks between their visits always drove him greedy, desperate to get all he could before he would have to face the teen again, sitting in his pews, right in front of him and forbidden.

Now, he was almost afraid to touch him. He could still feel the weight of Dante's head in his hands.

"Did... did you dream?" Dante asked, voice small and meek. Jude turned to him. "About me..."

For a moment, he considered lying. "Yes," Jude said.

Dante winced. His hands tightened around the mug. "Tell me what you saw. Please."

He shouldn't, Jude thought. He regarded Dante's stiff body, the poise of him sitting at his kitchen island, the creeping edge of panic on the teen's face. Sunlight painted over him from the window. Jude wished he could suspend Dante in this moment and keep it with him to carry, never having to face the next after he admitted what was already forming in his throat.

"I saw you in fire," Jude said. "I was there with you. And there was a voice."

"What did it say?"

Jude shook his head and silently crossed over to pull out a stool on the other side of the island, across from Dante, and sat down. He reached out and took Dante's hand, rubbing the back of it with his thumb. They were soft as always, the thin bones brittle under his fingers. Easy to break, Jude thought. Dante was always so easy to hurt. The dagger glinted in his memory, shimmering like molten silver.

"I'm not going to tell you that," Jude whispered.

Dante's mouth opened as if to protest, only to close. "Okay."

The lack of sleep, deep rest, was gnawing at them both. Jude let his eyes close, savoring the quiet morning, the warmth in the air. It was going to be a beautiful day, and Jude thought it felt wrong to follow after the wicked night.

"I... I had a dream too. Again," Dante muttered. "I've been having them."

"Did you?" Jude sat up. A dread crawled over

him. He had known that already, somehow. As soon as he had woken up and looked at Dante, he had known.

"It changes," Dante said. "But it's the same voice, every time. I'm in a desert and it's talking to me. It tells me I have to go..."

"...to Jerusalem," Jude finished.

Dante looked up at him wide-eyed. "To Jerusalem. Yeah. How..."

"What do you think?" Jude asked, meeting Dante's eyes with his own weary ones.

"I..." Dante's mouth dried, stunned, a tense fear creeping up his spine. He stared off for a moment before taking another mouthful of warm coffee, steeling himself.

"I'm in the desert, and sometimes I'm on a throne. The voice wants me to build it. Sometimes there's..." bodies ran through his head. The piles of them. The texture of their rotting skin, decomposing alongside live flesh, the thrashing ones left, smeared in the wet and dark viscera of the dead, slick with sweat under the beating sun. He thought of their voices, wailing so loud, so many of them, until the sound was not even human.

"...people," Dante finally said. "People who are there... because of me. For me. And then I hear these horns, getting louder and louder, until I finally just wake up."

Dante looked up to Jude. "What does it

mean?" Jude hesitated just long enough for Dante to laugh nervously, unable to stand the anxiety tightening around him, clawing into his chest. "It's only dreams, right?"

Jude thought of Joseph and his dream of the sun, the moon, and eleven stars bowing down. He thought of King Nebuchadnezzar and his dream of a statue in gold and silver and bronze and iron and clay and Daniel recounting a dream that was not his own, the ruin of the kingdom divined not by Daniel but told through him from an almighty spirit. He thought of the four dreams of Joseph and what they said of Mary and her child, how they warned him to flee to Egypt, away from the King who would slay them.

Countless dreams of countless kings and saints. Jude sat heavy in them all, thinking of his own and if there could be such a thing as just a dream for him. God had a way of talking. He had done it enough.

Like the same thoughts had crossed into him, Dante spoke again, panicked, leaning closer to Jude. "I can't be—"

"No," Jude said. "You aren't. It doesn't make sense."

The words seemed to ease Dante. He slumped back in his seat. Jude tried not to continue the thought and all the ways in which, maybe, it was all possible.

THEY HAD PARKED BEHIND THE LARGE OAK tree at the corner before Dante's house, off the road and hidden. Sunlight beamed and wavered between the shade of the leaves, tiny pinpoints of light. It was warm out, hot at the start of May.

"See you later this week?" Dante asked. One hand held his bag, his other already at the door handle to leave.

"Yeah," Jude said, before leaning over and gripping Dante's shoulders to pull him in and catch his mouth with his own, kissing him deep. Dante made a noise, flustered, bag slipping through his fingers.

In all their time, Jude had never kissed him outside of his house or office. He wouldn't so much as touch him when they were outside. Now Jude kissed him where anyone could see if they only walked by. The need in it was heavy, seeped bitterly into Dante's mouth.

Jude's hands came up to hold Dante by the back of his head, thumbs under his jaw, tilting Dante's face higher to him and holding him there. The sensation was familiar. As Jude kissed him, deeper still, he realized it felt exactly as it did in the dream when the same head sat in his hands, decapitated and bloody, cinnamon eyes beaming up in firelight.

When Jude pulled away, there was a strange and pained look in his eyes, one Dante had never seen before. It wasn't even guilt.

"I love you," Jude said as he let him go, settling back into his seat.

"Yeah..." Dante trailed off, still trying to figure out what it was about Jude that had changed. "I love you too."

He grabbed his bag again and finally stepped out of the car, waving goodbye at Jude as he steered back onto the road, headed back to his place where he would get ready to open the Church and carry on the day's service.

As the car disappeared into the red-streaked morning horizon, it occurred to Dante what that look had been in Jude.

It was fear.

JUDE WAS GOING TO COLLEGE ON A scholarship. Football had paid off after all those years in high school. It was a regular state college, nothing Ivy League, but it was a full ride. He would study humanities, get a bachelor's, and do a bit of traveling before returning home.

That was the plan. Then his dad got sick.

Irony would have led his dad to crumple at the pulpit, under God's eye, in God's house. That might have meant something, Jude thought. The intent would have been clear.

Instead, it was a calm Wednesday morning spent over breakfast when his dad suddenly seized, the whites of his eyes bright in the sun beaming in from the window, right before he collapsed from his chair and onto the hardwood floor.

It took him a moment to realize his dad was still alive on the ground and not just dead. God struck him down, Jude thought, staring at the still body. His kind dad, a devout man who never missed opening the town church in all thirty years of his service. Even though there was no reason for it to happen, not that he knew, it was Jude's first impulse. God wanted him dead.

Then his dad gripped his chest, gasped.

As Jude carried him out to his truck, tore through the old town's decrepit roads and sped towards the only hospital a half hour away, Jude asked God if he was going to kill his father that day.

Heart attack, the doctors later said. His dad lived, but he did not get lucky. It did damage, they explained. Cardiomyopathy.

The first night his dad was out of the hospital, he told Jude to have a drink with him. "We need to talk about the church," he said, solemn over their glasses of whiskey. It should have been exciting that his dad was letting him drink. It wasn't.

Jude's college acceptance letter had been received months ago. His things were near packed. He'd be moving into the dorms in just a few weeks.

"—And my retirement."

Later, Jude would be leaving the town, not for college, but ministry, at least a decade sooner than he had ever planned.

He didn't need to be the next pastor, technically. It was not a lineage. The pastor of the small town's local church did not need to be handed down in birthright. But his grandfather did it, his father did, and now he would on the pure fact they wanted it. The town wanted it.

Maybe God wanted it too. As soon as Jude told himself that, it all settled easily over him. He had read his bible close enough to know there were simply things that were done. He didn't have to worry about what he wanted.

In those years he followed that close, always acting as others wanted him to. All until Dante.

Give me one thing, he said to the bible on his nightstand as Dante slept next to him. *Give me one thing, out of all I give.*

Except that was never how it worked. He knew that.

Dante's mother was cooking. He sat at the dining table across from the kitchen, facing her as she stood at the stove. Spaghetti boiled in the pot. The room smelled like tomatoes and meat. It was eight P.M. and the sun had set, the apartment dark and cooling in its absence.

The small light above the stove had been turned on, casting her face in soft yellow. The thoughts swirling in his head seemed surreal in the moment. Something he knew to be true and yet impossible, and the idea that he had never been anything but the child who had lived here his whole life, born from only from a soft-handed mother.

"Mom," Dante said.

"Yes, Dante?"

"Do you know who my father is?"

Her hand stilled briefly, for a second. He might have missed it if he wasn't looking at her. "What do you mean?" She asked, face down to the stove. "Of course I do. He was my husband. I didn't know him long but—"

"I know you're lying."

She stopped stirring. Hesitantly, she set the

spoon to the side and turned to Dante. "Who told you?"

"Mrs. Walker."

"Jenny," she hissed. An arm crossed around her waist, her other hand coming up to press her fingers to her forehead. "Of course she did."

He wasn't sure what it was he had expected. Maybe a magic answer that explained it all. Further denial. Instead, a fundamental part of his mythology buckled under the slightest pressure.

"You... you've just been lying? For years?" Dante was surprised at the lack of anger behind it, how calm he sounded.

"I'm sorry, Dante," she said. "You asked when you were so little, I just... I couldn't tell you. And then I never knew what else to say."

"So, what actually happened?"

Dannie sighed, turned again to the stove. The pot was bubbling in an angry rush, steam rising up in ghost-like wisps. She turned it off and took it to the sink to drain. When it was empty, she set it aside and turned around to lean against the counter, facing her son.

"I had a very hard time before. When I was young. I used to spend all my time at the Mine."

The only local bar in the city. A small, shitty thing that the town crowded around. It's where people passing by spent their time, where teenagers snuck in and the sun-beaten men of the town planted themselves for hours each night.

"I would wait around," she said, "and then I'd go home with whoever wanted to take me. I didn't stop until I realized I was pregnant."

He should have been surprised. Part of him was. His mother had never so much as dated in his lifetime. It was strange to reconcile the idea with the Dannie he knew now, before him, standing in the kitchen in her soft mom jeans and half-sleeve shirt, even in the damp summer night.

"Do you even know who he was?"

"No, Dante. I have no idea."

He stiffened. Suddenly he felt feverish, sick, his face draining. As if he had forgotten how to breathe, his lungs merely stopped, and Dante had to struggle for another breath.

"Oh, Dante," she said, misunderstanding his reaction. "You saved me, baby. I stopped all of that. I got my GED, I started going to church. Pastor Raymond put in a word for me and I was able to get my job and take care of you."

Dante said nothing. After a moment, Dannie turned back to the stove to turn off the burner. Needlessly, she picked up the spoon and stirred the sauce again, face tilted down toward it.

"I haven't done anything like that since," she said.

Dante wasn't sure how to tell her he wouldn't have cared at all. She did nothing wrong, he thought. Nothing unlike what millions of people did every day, who went and had their own bastard children, all perfectly human and safe and blissfully unremarkable. There was no reason for Dannie, of them all, to have this kind of child.

Like him, she was only unfortunate.

JUDE HAD BEEN IGNORING HIM. WHEN DANTE had texted him a few days later, no reply came. It wasn't until Dante sent message after message, each more frantic than the last, devolving into *'are you alive?'* that Jude sent back one simple text.

'Fine.'

After that, Dante stopped messaging.

Youth group was Thursday night. It was the same group Dante had used to find so many excuses to talk to Jude alone, one-on-one for 'guidance' in his office until the day they both broke. When the meeting ended that night and Dante approached, Jude said he was late for something and rushed Dante out the door with everyone else, not even looking at him.

It was Sunday now.

Church used to be something of a game for them. Waiting until the others were bowed in prayer or to the choir to turn to each other and stare across the room, both wanting and wicked, Dante trying not to laugh and Jude trying not to hate himself.

That morning Dante looked up and not

once did he find Jude meeting him; the pastor's gaze turned down into the open bible and notes before him, sheltered behind his podium.

The service ended. The congregation lined up to head out the door, mingling with each other. Dante hung in the back of the crowd, waiting for the rest to trickle out.

Eventually there were only a few left. An older woman, Eloise from the clerk's office, was standing with Jude. Clarissa, her pretty blonde granddaughter in blue jean shorts that revealed the skin of long, smooth legs, stood beside her, smiling up at him. She was in her twenties, nearly Jude's own age. A soft-spoken country girl like all the girls Jude had ever dated before. It was not the first time Clarissa had lingered back to speak to Jude, laughing with a voice like bells at every other thing he said.

Dante was close enough to hear Eloise's teasing voice. "You know, pastors are allowed to marry, Jude, and there're so many lovely girls right here."

"Oh, I know, and I would be so honored," he said, smiling politely at Clarissa. "Unfortunately, it is not part of the plan for now."

The words soothed Dante, sinking into his coiled nerves. It was strange how Jude never dated anyone else, he thought, even though their relationship was secret, essentially nonexistent. It was a loyalty Dante had never asked for, and yet Jude gave it to him all the same.

The two women gave their goodbyes and left, only for someone else to step up.

"Honey," Dannie said. She had just finished speaking to the neighbors and was at Dante's side now, hand gently squeezing his shoulder. "You ready to go?"

"No," Dante said. "I have to talk to Pastor Jude. You should go home, mom. I'll get a ride after."

She frowned. "Everything okay?" Dante nodded and she sighed, ruffling his hair. "Alright, baby. I'll see you soon, then. Let me know if you want me to pick you up later."

"Okay," he said, and Dannie squeezed his shoulder one more time before heading out.

When she was done, Dante went up to Jude's side, ignoring the woman he was talking to. "Pastor," Dante said, voice tight. "Can I speak with you after this?"

The look Jude gave him was cutting, a rare and true irritation that Jude rarely ever showed. Dante was pleased all the same, like he had won something.

"Of course," Jude said, voice low and careful, a pseudo calm. The woman looked down at Dante as if just noticing him. Dante was still turned to Jude when she started speaking.

"Dante, bestia de scorto natus."

It wasn't the first time he heard tongues. It took Dante a moment to realize she had even switched languages. When he turned to her, he flinched under the beady, intense gaze of her eyes, as if it burned through him. The woman in front of him no longer resembled the person he had seen so often each Sunday, now drained of expression, pupils swelled in her eyes like pits. Almost inhuman.

Jude tensed beside him. "*Tua imago erit colitur ab hominibus et damnabit eos,*" she hissed. "*Vade in Ierusalem.*"

Her head snapped to Jude. "*Jude, occide Dante.*"

Cold terror slid through Jude all at once, his jaw tight. It would have been hard for anyone to tell he was anything but a man listening curiously, the fear of it slipped safe under his skin.

All at once the compulsion stopped. Dante and Jude looked on in quiet sick horror as something left the woman, her own self hazily rising back. Her eyes shrank down, her eyebrows cinched as if from a headache. Gingerly she touched her forehead. "That was so strange," she said, distant.

"I..." she looked to Jude, alarmed. "I don't know what I said, Pastor. Why don't I know it?"

With one sharp look to Dante, a warning that told the teen to stay, Jude took her shoulder and walked with her to the door. "Because you are not always meant to know. Some things are just felt."

Thoughtless, she let him guide her, pausing at the door he held open. "Did it make any sense to you, Pastor?"

"Ah, yes," Jude said. "It was, 'You are my child, made in my image, and I am with you. Walk in peace.'"

She looked back at Dante, still standing off to the side, muted panic sharp inside him and wondering if it was all too obvious on his face.

"Did I not say Dante's name?"

"Did you?" Jude said. "Perhaps I missed that. I am so sorry but I have to attend to something now."

There were more people still in the church. Just a few, but they lingered, their voices soft in the wide-open room.

Jude turned to Dante. "Go to my office."

"Jude?"

"Now." As if just realizing the others could hear him snapping, he softened his voice. "Please."

Jude was already turned away from him, heading to the others. With nothing left to do, Dante slowly made his way across the church and to the hall, down the length of it to the room he had become so familiar with, as if he had a claim to the space just as much as Jude.

Dante stepped in and shut the wooden door

behind him softly, breath ragged now that he was alone and safe, able to let the tension move through him.

After some time had passed, enough to let people finish their conversations and say their goodbyes, the pack of them finally headed out of the church and into their cars to drive off into the bright light of the day. The door opened and Jude stepped in.

Silently, the man went to his desk, settling at his chair. Dante sat across, waiting. Jude looked tired, Dante thought. Tension ran through the man and sank into Dante himself, though he refused to show it.

Finally, Jude spoke. "She was speaking Latin."

Jude knew Latin. Dante remembered when he began to study it years ago, before he went to ministry. On rare tiffs between them, Jude would even switch to Latin, teasing Dante with things unknown, riling him up until Dante would scream. Jude had always started laughing then, until Dante laughed back.

Dante didn't feel like laughing now. "What did she say?"

Jude would not look at him, his face bitterly turned down to the desk. "She said, 'Dante, beast born of a whore, your image will be worshipped by the people and it will damn them. Go to Jerusalem.'"

"It's—she's faking," Dante insisted with an edge of panic. "Right? Jude? She has to be. I can't..."

"Why would she?" Jude asked, voice dark and solemn. He would not meet Dante's eyes, staring down to the floor instead. "Do you think she gave you those dreams too?"

There was another sentence she had said. One Jude kept safe and hidden under his tongue. *Jude, you will slay Dante.*

"So that means I'm..." Dante trailed off, stunned, afraid of saying another thing. He was suddenly afraid of being in the office. In his own skin. His body seeped with sick terror, spine chilling as if someone was behind him. He wanted to hide somewhere. He wanted to press his back into Jude's form, as if Jude could save him from anything.

"That's why..." Jude laughed, low and bitter. "I was so guilty when all this time, I've just been fucking the Antichrist."

Dante's head snapped up to him, eyes wide.

"Does that make you feel better?" Dante bit. He crossed his arms, took a step back. "Is everything suddenly okay if I'm evil? Can you do no wrong to me?" Dante thought of that first kiss that happened in this room. The wall that Jude had pinned him to was just in the corner of his eye now, haunting. He thought of Jude's mouth harsh against his, the sharp teeth of the man, large hands gripping him until he bruised.

Who moved first? He couldn't remember.

Jude's deep brown eyes finally rose to meet Dante's. For a moment, he was silent. Dante's gut coiled as he waited. Jude had never looked at him like that before. Calculated and cold, suspicious. Repulsed. He regarded him like Dante was a snake that had wandered into his house, the quiet recognition before leaving to grab a shotgun.

"Have you compelled me?" Jude asked.

Dante glared. "I don't know, *Pastor.* Have you strayed so much that you could be compelled?" Heat stung his eyes, tears slowly welling in them and dripping over his face. He wasn't sure what was more sickening. That Jude wanted to blame him for all that had happened, or that Jude thought it was possible he didn't care about Dante after all. That he wanted everything between them to just be an illusion he did not will.

Jude watched him cry for a moment, silent and unmoving. The air in the room was stale, cold and dark in shadow, only lit by the dim fluorescent bulb above. "No."

He stood up from his desk and crossed over to him, reaching out to touch Dante's hair. His hand drifted over his jaw, to his cheek, slow motions that lulled Dante to even breaths.

Jude's thumb wiped the streak of tears from his eye. "No, Dante. I'm here. I'm still with you."

When Dante flung himself into Jude, arms tight to his waist and face hidden against his chest, Jude held him softly and tried to see the figure that was wrapped so tight around him as the Antichrist. The Beast. Enemy.

All he could see was Dante, a thin and familiar form clinging to him with raw need, trying and failing to muffle the steady sounds of his gutted sobbing, each cry breaking something inside of Jude a little more.

J̇UDE, YOU WILL SLAY DANTE, AND THE BEAST will rise with a mortal wound upon its head, and you will carry him to Jerusalem and he will sit on the throne of Solomon, and the people will worship his image.

Jude, you will slay Dante.

Slay Dante.

Jude woke to a pitch-black room. The air was still, softened only by the distant sound of crickets and the rustle of trees outside.

Dante slept next to him. Jude turned to his figure, gravitating to the warmth of him. His eyes slowly adjusted to the soft haze of the moonlight that seeped in from the window until he could make out Dante's form, lying peacefully beneath the cover.

It was hard to imagine Dante was what God had told him. A tool for the end of days. In this hour, alone and quiet, hidden away in the shadows of the night with nothing between them but their own breathing, it was hard to imagine Dante was anything but his own.

Slowly, to not disturb him, Jude shifted closer to Dante. He reached out and pulled the blanket down to expose Dante's back, the skin of it prickling at the cool night air sweeping over. Jude's fingertips traced down the sharp curve of his spine, nails ghosting over the surface. Absent-mindedly, Jude drew patterns over the skin, his fingers skittering over the expanse of Dante's shoulder blade and down to the small dip of his lower back.

Even in the dark night, Jude could make out the deep, angry bruises forming across Dante's body from what he had done to him earlier that evening.

Jude wondered if his cruel aggression against Dante came from some innate place inside of him, like maybe he always knew. Maybe this was always meant to be his role.

He took Dante's shoulder and gently pulled him over so he was lying on his back, face tilted up and throat exposed. Jude rested his hand over the column of it and gently squeezed. Could he do it? If the mission was to kill Dante, if that was what he had to do, could he?

The feel of Dante's throat in his palm reminded Jude of the time he hit a deer. When he pulled over and got out of the car, he had found it mangled on the side of the road, still alive. It had screamed at him through its broken bones, its blood and viscera smeared across the asphalt. It was a terrible ungodly sound, so loud it seemed impossible for anything so damaged to be able to make. But it did.

Being raised in his small rural town, Jude had been taught to hunt. He had shot deer before with his father out in the forest during the game seasons. He would have shot the deer withering in front of him except he didn't carry his shotgun in his car.

It was suffering. For a moment Jude wondered if he should just drive away, as if to shrink back from the idea his mind had started to curl around. Or, he thought he wanted to be the kind of person who wanted to drive away, as if not having to kill it would be a relief to him. Except he didn't really want to run.

Jude stood over the animal and took an antler in each hand, the velvet of them not yet shed. It was soft against his hands, warm. With one quick jerk, Jude snapped its neck and let go, its head falling limp onto the ground. It was finally quiet.

The act had been easier than he thought, even as he felt the resistance of the neck in his hands, the snap of bone running through the antlers and up his arms.

Dante couldn't be much harder.

Jude squeezed a little more, fingers pressing firmly into the tender meat under him. He could feel the muscle of the neck, the soft heartbeat against his hand.

With a shuddering sigh, Dante shifted, his pupils moving beneath his eyelids. He turned and instead of struggling out of Jude's hold, he leaned into the man, pressing himself deeper into his open hand.

Jude choked, breathless at how Dante curled close to rest in the crook of his shoulder, so loving, so wanting of him even like this. Jude let go. His arms wrapped around Dante instead to pull him in closer.

Maybe he could kill Dante. If that's what he needed to do, was told to do, maybe he could in the same way Abraham could lead Isaac up the mountain. In this moment though, he was awake and the voice was gone. Dante rested in his arms. This moment in the cool dark night was theirs, and theirs alone. For right now, Jude thought, Dante belonged only to him.

IN THE MORNING THE TWO OF THEM MET IN the kitchen, Dante taking his familiar seat at the island. Jude placed a mug of coffee in front of him, made the same way he always did, mindful of exactly what Dante liked. Dante took it gratefully in both hands, so warm it almost hurt. He let it sooth him, even in the humid, damp morning of oncoming summer heat.

Jude stepped back to lean against the

counter, arms crossed. "God told me to kill you."

Dante's eyes flicked up to him. He said nothing.

"That's what my dreams are, Dante. That's all I hear in them."

"Do you want to?"

"Don't ask me that." Jude flexed his fist and imagined Dante's throat in it again.

"You'll set off the entire thing, you know," Dante said. He was casual as he spoke, like they weren't talking about his death. Talking about Jude being the one to do it.

"It's going to happen," Jude said. "It's supposed to happen." A necessary step. One event in a long list of some greater plan.

"I do not want to be the one to make it happen," Dante bit. "I do not want to condemn the world with my own existence! You're asking me to bring stupid sheep to slaughter."

"I'm not asking anything, Dante."

Dante looked at him silently, the cold horror of the truth sitting between them in the room, unspoken but ever present, so heavy Dante thought it might drag him straight down to the pit of the earth.

DANTE WOKE UP IN THE MIDDLE OF THE night. Jude slept on peacefully next to him, the soft sound of his breathing filling the room. Dante had spent the night again, was doing it more often. At some point his mother would begin to question why he was at his friend's house so much. Until then, he only wanted to be here. Dante looked down at the man and brushed some of his blond hair back. He wondered if Jude was dreaming of killing him now.

Moonlight painted the room in a deep blue, dream-like. He thought he should go back to sleep, except he was tired of hearing that voice and the things it showed him.

Silent, Dante shuffled out of the covers and stepped out of the bed, walking out of the room and through the backdoor.

LATER IN THE NIGHT, JUDE WOKE TO FIND himself alone. He was so used to sleeping by himself that it took him a few moments to realize that Dante had spent the night with him and should have been there.

Jude wandered around his house looking for him. Each room met him with only a stunning silence. Jude gazed out the front, thinking maybe Dante had driven off, except Jude's car was still there and Dante did not have his own.

It may have been possible Dante called his mom to pick him up, except Jude knew Dante would never. There was a fierceness in Dante that made him as defensive of Jude as Jude was afraid of being revealed.

Lost, Jude paced through his house again when a light from his back window caught his eye. He came to it and looked outside to see the church, yards from the house. Soft light, hazy from across the dark grounds, illuminated from inside.

Jude opened the backdoor and stepped onto the ground, barefoot. Dew clung to him as he walked through wet grass, cold on his feet. In a few minutes Jude was across the yard and at the church door.

He found Dante inside, sitting in the front pew.

The lights were off, but Dante had lit candles, dozens of them, strewn across the front of the church.

It was so unlike the fluorescents they used during the day. The light cast over the church in a dim, flickering glow, and everything it hit was painted a little more red.

The cross that hung in the front was cloaked in shadows and Jude stilled, taken back by how much larger it seemed in the dark, more foreboding and divine. The spirit was everywhere at all times; that was what Jude said in their sermons. And yet now, looking up, he felt as if it pressed down on him in a way it never had before: undeniable. The sculpted eyes of the wooden Jesus burned through him.

He made his way to the front and quietly took a seat next to Dante. The teen's head was bowed down, head resting on his clasped hands.

"Are you praying?" Jude asked. He remembered, suddenly, when he was a small child and would pray to thank God for Satan, so that someone would tempt the unworthy and the stupid away, before he grew up and learned how to hold shame for his hate. How strange now, to sit across from that same entity's child.

"I was thinking."

Dante lifted his head to gaze up at the cross hanging above. Jude followed his eyes, looking up with him. Some of the crucifixions in other churches were made so beautiful, without so much as an edge of blood, a full and healthy chest, bright wondrous eyes.

Their own, brought in by Jude's grandpa decades ago when he was running the church, did not shy away from any of it. Red paint ran down from pierced hands and nails. Each rib was outlined as if pulled taut against the skin, the body emaciated. There was no mistaking the expression as anything but a man who was dying.

Jude glanced back at Dante, who stayed transfixed, face tilted up. In the back of his head, Jude thought he looked too beautiful in the haze of the candlelight. Untouchable, pristine. Like he was blessed. Like he could be holy.

"Are you afraid of being sacrificed like that?" Jude asked. *Slay Dante.*

"No," he said. "I'm jealous." He turned to Jude. "Jesus had it easy. He was meant to save them."

Jude wasn't expecting that. "You want to be staked to a cross and tortured until you die?"

"To stop the end of times?" Dante asked, huffing with a bitter smile. "I'd let you destroy me. I'd give any suffering."

He spoke with such sincerity, misery dripping in his voice, that Jude believed him. Of course, he thought. That was exactly the kind of person Dante was. Always had been. For a moment, Jude was there with Dante, understood what he meant and agonized all the same. If there was anything he could have done to change things, to make it better for him, to take his place, he would have. But they were only themselves, helpless parts of a game far beyond the two of them.

Jude reached out and pulled Dante in tenderly, arms wrapped around as if he were something Jude could keep. "So suffer."

For the next few weeks, they waited. Jude poured over revelations and tried to glean more clues, a better timeline. Anything to indicate what was supposed to happen, come next. If Dante did not want to do this and took no action, Jude did not understand how the rest followed.

It was a form of denial, really. The dreams were becoming more frantic, incessant. Always when Dante was in his bed, when he so much as faded off on the couch next to him during a movie.

Jude, you will slay Dante, and the beast will rise, and you will carry him to Jerusalem, and he will sit on the throne of Solomon.

Jude, you will slay Dante, and the beast will rise, and you will carry him to Jerusalem, and he will sit on the throne of Solomon.

Jude, you will slay Dante, and the beast will rise, and you will carry him to Jerusalem, and he will sit on the throne of Solomon.

He knew what came next.

Their visits with each other were closer and closer together, both craving the other like it was relief. Dante brought Jude the dreams but for Dante, they never stopped. It wasn't hard for Jude to deal with it, if it meant Dante was at least not alone when waking.

Sometimes Jude entertained the thoughts. When he and Dante were in the kitchen talking, Jude's attention would drift to the knife block on the counter. What would it be like to take one out and ram it into the back of Dante's head, right at the junction of his neck and skull? Once Jude did take one out and walked around the kitchen with it, just to see if Dante would notice. He didn't. Jude ended up slicing an apple with it for them to share.

It was weeks of pretending the next step wasn't due when Dante showed up at Jude's door on a weekday night, unannounced. The sky was already pitch-black when Jude opened the door to see Dante under the foggy yellow glow of his porch light, moths and June bugs bumping against the glass fixture.

"I didn't realize you were coming over," Jude said, before opening the door all the way and heading into the kitchen, silently encouraging Dante to come in before he could get a word out.

Dante sighed and shut the door behind him, following Jude.

They stood in the kitchen across from each other. A glass of water was set out at Dante's usual spot on the island. Dante noted the whiskey bottle on the counter and a short glass, a thin trace of the liquor left inside.

He didn't take his seat. "I came to say goodbye."

"Goodbye?" Jude scoffed and crossed his arms. Anxiety cinched in his throat. "And where would you be going?"

"Somewhere, away from here." Dante said. Though Dante was 5'8", only a few inches shorter than Jude, the teen suddenly looked so much smaller as he flinched into himself, head tipped to the floor.

"Somewhere," Jude mocked. "And why are you going, Dante?"

Dante didn't answer. Jude waited for a beat and when the stubbornness did not break, air stiff in the room, he crossed the kitchen to stand in front of him. He tucked a piece of hair behind his ear and noted how Dante shivered. "Well?"

"Jude," Dante choked. "You need to stop."

"Stop what?"

"Seeing me!" Dante flinched away. "Being with me, talking to me—all of it!" Every night together Dante had seen Jude's edges slipping a little more, the twitch of his face when he slept. The longer he stayed with Jude, the more the man had to defy that voice. The less he could rest. The more Dante risked Jude taking up the command.

It was only now Dante had really begun to interrogate the seams of their relationship. Even if he wasn't what he was, he had pulled Jude down enough with him. He wondered how much it mattered who moved first in the office that night, when Dante was the one who had been circling Jude around like a dog, closer and closer until one of them could lunge.

"I'm not good for you," Dante whimpered. He never had been.

Jude glared down. "Don't tell me what's good for me, Dante."

"Jude, I—"

"You are not leaving." That wasn't the plan for them, Jude told himself, as if that was the only reason for his protest.

Dante's jaw snapped shut. His eyebrows furled, glaring right back. It was the first time Dante had looked at Jude all night. The cinnamon of his eyes glittered and Jude wondered if there wasn't truly an ember of hellfire behind them. "We'll, I'm not doing this either," Dante bit.

"How many times do I have to say it's not up to you?" Jude said, voice low and dark. He gripped Dante's arms, his hands hard like steel around him, and pushed him until the island's countertop was digging into his back, the edge painful against his spine. "It's going to happen, Dante." An uncomfortable anger had seeped into him. A horrible, red-hot impulse that spiked through and made him want to rip something. Distantly, Jude considered how strange it was to feel this much rage at Dante, of all people.

"Jude, let me go," Dante said. He sounded firm, even as he struggled with futile effort. There was no getting out of Jude's grip. He should have known that by now with how often Jude held him down in bed, but he supposed he had never really tried to escape. He was realizing now exactly how much strength was behind Jude's thick arms, how his own skinny ones were helpless against it. His heart quickened and he tried to twist again, only for Jude to squeeze harder, fingers digging in and bruising all the way to the bone. Dante yelped.

"So you can run away to the middle of nowhere? Get yourself killed anyways?" He saw Dante's body smeared on a dark road in the middle of the mountains. He saw strangers finding Dante at the wrong time of night with a gun, or pulling up beside him in their car, offering a ride only to take him away to where he'd never be seen again. Jude saw every terrible demise that Dante could meet, painful and aching thoughts, and the worst of all was he wasn't there in a single one. If it was inevitable,

Jude thought, then it should at least be his own hands. "No."

"I won't let you," Dante said, his voice brittle like he was crying, but there were no tears yet. "Jude, I can't let you do this—I can't let this happen. It shouldn't be you, I'm so sorry."

He had stopped struggling. Dante stood slack between the counter and Jude's body, his breath hitching. Jude waited and after a moment, when Dante was still pliant in his grip, his hand came to rest on Dante's throat.

Dante swallowed hard, the sensation moving against Jude's palm, but he did not resist. *Maybe I should just do it now*, Jude thought. It would be easy enough. He squeezed and Dante's mouth parted, breath spilling from him. "Jude," he whispered.

The sound, the pleading, snapped something inside of the man. It rose to call and Jude leaned in to press his forehead to Dante's own. *Do it now*, he thought, fingernails scraping over the skin of Dante's throat, the teen's rabbit-quick pulse under his fingers. *Now, now*. Jude leaned in and brushed his mouth against Dante's.

The grip slackened. Dante kissed Jude back, mouth dry and firm, more than familiar. When the man's breathing had slowed, when his hands slipped from Dante's throat to his shoulders instead, Dante took his chance. He shoved Jude from him with all the force he could give, forcing Jude to stumble back. Dante bolted for the front door across the room.

He wasn't fast enough. Jude snatched him by the wrist and yanked him back, Dante nearly falling.

"You have to let me go!" He screamed. "Jude!"

"I do not obey you!" Jude yelled back. Dante struggled in his grip, twisting and yanking, a wildness in his eyes like fire blazing. It only pissed Jude off more and in a flash of rage, unthinking, vicious, only wanting it all to stop, Jude gripped the length of Dante's silk black hair and slammed his head down into the hard corner of the island's stone countertop.

A crack split loud against the surface. Dante's head gave, slumping in.

There was no struggle anymore. The teen's body went limp, soundless, and when Jude let go of his hair, he fell to the ground.

Blood dripped from the corner of the countertop in a steady, delicate rhythm. More flowed from the open wound in the middle of his forehead, pooling across the wooden floor. There was broken skin there, edges of split bone, and a thick, pale matter that Jude didn't want to consider. He dropped to the floor, crouching by what was left of the teen.

"Dante? Dante?" There was no response. Jude watched his chest, waiting for some sign of rise and fall only to see none. He was suddenly sick.

Dante was dead.

Staring at the body bleeding out in his own kitchen, under the pale yellow lights and dark night staring in at them from the windows, Jude had a terrible thought for a moment that dreams were only that, terrible dreams, and there was no God's voice speaking to him. There was no rite to carry out.

Dante was not the Antichrist. He was just a seventeen-year-old from the church, dead on Jude's floor.

"Please," Jude rasped, tears swelling hot and stinging in his eyes.

Dante, nor God, had any kind of response.

JUDE SET HIM IN THE BATHTUB WHILE HE cleaned the kitchen, scrubbing up the blood that had started to soak into the flooring. He discovered more fragments of bones on the counter, slivers stuck in bits of flesh, and found himself thinking of nothing at all. Not Dante, dead in the bathroom. Not God, not his dreams, not his father who had walked across these very floors before Jude came to them, not the church and the town, not Dante's mother. He thought of nothing and cleaned.

He finished late in the night. Dante's body had drained out in the tub, red streaked all over the porcelain surface. Jude washed him gently in warm water and when he was finished drying, wrapped him up in a white sheet that smelled of cedar, lingering from the chest he pulled it from.

There were a few places he could put the body. The attic upstairs, the shed outside. Beneath the house. Even in the church itself, hidden in the crawlspace.

In the end, there was only one place Jude could stand. Tenderly he held Dante's body, so much heavier than it ever had been, and carried him into the bedroom. Jude set him under the bed, pushed into the deep center where no one could see.

That night he lay alone, opened-eyed, tranquilized by the acute knowledge that Dante rested just below him.

There was a sermon the next day. Jude considered asking his dad to fill in for him, saying he was sick, but he ended up getting dressed and opened the church himself anyway.

The service went on as normal. Dannie was missing. Jude's attention drifted to her and Dante's empty seat again and again, but if anyone noticed, they did not say anything. *Do you know?* Jude wanted to ask his congregation. His neighbors, the old women he had seen at the church since he was just a child, families and their own children, his father sitting in the front row. *Do you know what I've done? Did God give you dreams too?* Jude read from his notes, only a small, fractured part of him speaking, the rest of him under his bed with Dante.

When he got home, it was late. He went to the room and stared at the bed, hoping when he peered down that it would be empty. It would mean what Dante had feared and yet Jude wanted it, needed it, as long as it meant Dante would rise back.

Jude crouched down to see Dante's form still

wrapped in those white sheets, unmoving, cool in the shadow of the bed. In the morning, he found the same.

ON THE SECOND DAY OF DANTE'S DEATH, JUDE
went back to the church. Before the sermon had
started, Dannie found him in his office. "Dante's
been missing for two nights now," she said. Her
eyes were puffy, rimmed in red, and Jude
thought they looked like his own. "Pastor, can
you pray for him? Please?"

"I'm so sorry, Dannie," he said. "I can't
imagine how you're feeling. Yes, we will pray for
Dante's safe return." He had stood up from his
desk to take her hand, holding it as if to assure
her. He had done what he was supposed to do,
he reminded himself. What he had been
ordered to do. And yet, as he noted how similar
Dannie's hand felt to Dante's, he wondered if he
would burn anyway.

The congregation prayed. Dannie cried
beneath the sound of them, hidden in her lonely
pew, the empty spot by her stark in its negative
space. It was strange to talk about Dante as if he
were only a teen from the church he knew the
way he knew all of them, polite and distant.
Jude wouldn't so much as shake Dante's hand in

public and here he was, leading a prayer for the person he might have loved the most in his life, trembling alone in the grief at the front of his church, so subtle that his congregation would never see.

Dante was still under the bed when Jude returned home. *Three days,* he thought. Jesus too did not rise instantly. Why would Dante be any different? Jude told himself if Dante didn't rise by tomorrow, he wasn't going to. It would mean Dante was dead, truly dead, and he would need to hand the body over. Turn himself in.

As Jude laid down to sleep again, he considered the most horrifying part of it all was that since Dante was dead, Jude didn't have a single dream.

In the morning, Dante was still there. Perfectly still, the blood and skin of him all obscured in the white sheet. It was almost easy to pretend it wasn't a corpse, Jude thought. Like it was only a bundle he could leave under the bed, as if it would never change.

But it was a body, and it was not his to hoard. Jude pulled him out and lifted him into his arms. Rigor mortis had passed and Dante was limp, pliable. *How are you so heavy*, Jude wondered. Dante had felt weightless all the other times Jude had ever picked him up to carry and toss around. Now Dante weighed like he was made of stone, a marble figure.

There were woods in the back of his house, further down from the property line of the church. There was no service yet. No one would be out where he could be seen for hours. For now, he was alone and safe in the privacy of the back field, a piece of land passed through his family that he had inherited, a yard that his grandfather once overlooked, his father, and then him with Dante by his side.

He carried the body through the grass and into the dense cluster of trees, walking deep, deeper, until he was in the forest of the town and could not recognize the land. Like in the house, Jude was not sure where to leave him. He could just lay Dante down now, right on the floor of the forest, except that seemed too easy for something to wander along and eat him.

Eventually after searching, Jude came across a jutting stone. The space under it sheltered the ground in cool shade, other rocks circling around and shielding it. It reminded him of a cave, somewhere dark and quiet.

For a moment, Jude considered taking Dante back with him, hiding him under the bed until it rotted and maybe even past that. How long could he keep a dead boy in his house before someone found out?

Don't, he told himself. This place was as good as any. Jude knelt down and gently laid Dante against the cool rocks, damp from condensation, the smell of earth heavy and sweet. Jude cupped the side of Dante's face, cloaked by the sheet, one last time before he stood and started back for the house.

ON THE FOURTH DAY, THE BODY WAS FOUND.

A hunter's dog had picked up the smell and led his people over. Jude heard the news in the morning from the TV playing in the background. He should feel scared, he realized, as the description of Dante's body came over.

...body had been wrapped... head trauma... suspected missing teen, Dante Williams, reported missing by his mother, Dannette Williams, three days ago...

Instead, Jude was relieved he had been found so fast. His mother would have him again and he would be buried, not lost in the woods, eventually eaten away by animals and worms, his body nothing more than a place snakes came to settle in.

Jude attended service. The shock of the news had infested and exhausted his congregation, everyone forlorn with the news. People talked only in whispers, hesitant. They did not look into each other's eyes. Everyone settled into the pews and it was quiet, so quiet, more than should be possible for a room with so many people. *I can hear my heartbeat,* Jude thought, the sound thrumming under his skin.

Dannie was there again. Sitting alone, eyes bloodshot, gaze hazy and unfocused.

"I'm sure you've all heard," Jude said. "A terrible thing has happened today. A member of our church this morning..." His throat seized. His eyes stung. "Dante Williams, has passed on —" *I killed him* "—from us." *I killed him, I killed him, I took him from this Church and into my home I killed him he was under my bed he was in my bed.* Could they see him shaking? Jude gripped the podium so hard his fingers turned numb. "But we must remember in this time... there is a plan beyond us..." *God told me to, he did, I thought he did but now I don't know and where is God now? He was not with us in that room. Was that God? He was not there with us. God are you here? Areyouhereareyouhereareyouhere?*

The congregation stared patiently at him, even the small children quiet and still. Their parents had draped an arm over their shoulders. Some hugged them close. Dannie's lone figure stood out only harsher, the empty seat a beacon blinding him in its brutal, unyielding absence.

Jude did not notice the tears that overflowed and slipped down his face. "We all end... when God wants us back." *That's a lie. I ended him.*

I want him back.

Jude's breath hitched, a deep sob. "And if we

stay with faith... as Dante had..." *Dante was a rebel. Dante did not obey. Dante was so much better than I ever was and I killed him.* "One day, we will see him again—" Jude choked on the last word. He was sobbing now, the church echoing with the ugly agony of his crying.

The congregation looked at each other, hesitant, tense in the thick discomfort that ran through them. They had never seen their pastor break down. They had never seen Jude cry.

As much as he tried to talk again, the sobbing only continued, so hard he folded onto the podium, face hidden in his crooked arm. His tears and spit smeared onto the open bible and his notes below, the ink running over and staining both.

When it was apparent their pastor was beyond words, something in him broken, his father stood up and made his way to the front of the church. He put a hand on Jude's back. "Go home," he said. He didn't know what was wrong with Jude. He couldn't understand how the death of someone he barely knew, no matter how horrible, would wrack his son to this. But it hurt him all the same. "Jude, go home. I'll finish."

Jude nodded. It was only when his breathing had steadied that he stood again and walked through the middle of the aisles and to the doors without looking at or speaking to a single soul as if they weren't even there, heading out and across the grass to his own home, the tears still streaming.

On the fifth day, Jude stayed home again.

On the sixth day, someone knocked on the door.

It was early in the morning, when dawn just started to spill golden light. The grass and trees of his yard glimmered in the rays. The birds sang.

Jude was still in bed, although he had been awake for hours already. When he heard the knock, he considered ignoring it. Anyone from the church would only be there to offer him some baked sweet and glib words of comfort. It might have been his dad, in which case he should answer but would be forgiven for not. He could always call him later.

It occurred to him on the second knock, louder, that it might have been Dannie. He was the pastor, right? He owed her his responsibility, at least, to listen to her and provide comfort. He could do that little.

He dragged himself out of bed, threw on a shirt and went to the door to answer.

STANDING THERE AT THE DOORSTEP, SUNLIGHT beaming all over his dark black hair, halo-like, was Dante.

His Dante. Very much alive and looking up at Jude with his sparkling, wicked eyes, glaring. They looked different, Jude realized. The cinnamon color was brighter, more like raw rubies. Staring into them, he thought they shined eerily similar to the ones from his dreams, when firelight danced across them.

His head was no longer caved in. A fresh red scar marked Dante's forehead, its edges burst out from the center of the wound. Like a star, Jude thought.

"Jude," Dante growled, stepping in. He closed the door behind him, Jude too stunned to do anything.

"Dante, you're..."

"Alive?" Dante asked, sneering.

"No," Jude said, stunned. "You're... you really are the Antichrist."

Jude could have laughed, or cried. A thousand urges flooded him, crowded up into his throat until he felt like he was choking. "I was right after all," he gasped. "I was fucking right."

"Yes, and you saw to that, didn't you?"

Jude paused, like he just realized Dante was not only alive but alive and pissed, ready to fight. It was a strange look on him, this new reborn form. His Dante had always been kind, even in his anger.

"Dante," Jude said carefully. "I was only doing wha—"

"What you were *told?* Yes, you did, Jude." Dante stalked up to him and Jude found his breath leaving him as this form leaned in close, their faces inches apart. Jude marveled at the fury he carried, ache swelling in him even now for this angry, righteous, beautiful Dante.

"You were a *good man,* weren't you, Jude?" Dante hissed. "A true man of your God, ready to slaughter your own kind on command. So ready to slaughter *me.* Tell me, are you grateful you were the one asked to do it?"

"Stop it."

"No," Dante said, teeth bared. "No, you listened, Jude. And now you will listen to me."

"I do not follow you," Jude said. He stayed in place, close enough to feel Dante's breath on his face, waiting.

Dante huffed. "If you are not mine then rebuke me."

"I already did."

"Then do it again!" Dante screamed, the sound almost painful, echoing over the walls of the room. Jude winced but stayed. Dante took a trembling breath, centering himself. He spoke again, voice softer. "Rebuke me, Jude."

Jude opened his mouth again, only to shut it. The words sat behind his tongue, too weak to make their way out. Hadn't he done his job? Did he not already obey? There was nothing further he could give, he realized. He had already killed him.

And now Dante was here again. The relief, the manic want, was enough that Jude could collapse right there at his feet, if only Dante would stay there for him to rest under. He'd do anything, if only Dante would stay there.

"Dante," Jude whispered. "Please..."

Dante considered him, eyes flickering back and forth. The rage seemed to slip off in quiet contemplation, some dark mercy rolling over and stilling him. He raised his hands to hold Jude's face, leaning up closer to him.

He was warm, Jude realized. A small part of him wondered if he would still be dead and cold, but blood coursed through him like anything else alive, the heat of his fingers flushing over Jude's cheeks. It felt like it always had, the touch unmistakable. This was his Dante, still. Jude's eyelids fluttered, closing in bliss. When Dante leaned in and put his mouth to his, there was nothing else he could do but lean in deeper, chasing the taste.

He was supposed to love God above all, right? Except now, Jude knew there was nothing he loved more than Dante.

Eventually Dante pulled back. He stroked Jude's face with gentle fingers, raw affection dripping from him. "You are mine, Jude, aren't you?"

To say no would hurt. So Jude kept his mouth closed, saying nothing at all.

"Give me your hand."

For a moment, Jude hesitated. Then he lifted his hand and let Dante take it. He turned it over and brought it to his mouth, kissing the tender palm. Jude's fingers twitched under the sensation, Dante's soft mouth singeing against delicate nerves of the skin.

Dante pulled back and Jude looked to see a mark there now, red and dark like a bruise, mouth-shaped.

"Devil!" Jude hissed.

"You knew that." Dante rubbed at it, his thumb rolling over the mark. Gently at first, then rougher, digging into the pastor's hand so deep he could feel the muscle and sinew tense beneath. The mark remained.

That was it, then. The final proof. Dante suddenly felt sick and cold all over. The realization of what he had done to Jude settled over him, and he wasn't sure if the agony inside him was for the man or if he was pleased that if he got to mark anyone, it was Jude.

Did that mean that at the end of the world —at the end of themselves—Jude would be his to keep?

Yes, Jude would have said.

"The Miracle of Darkwood." That's what they were calling Dante. In the news, in the town.

Dante had been dead. There was no hiding that when the body was found, skull collapsed in, brain wet and leaking, head a glittering dome of ants when the dog had come across him. He had been sitting at the morgue. His mother had seen the body and had started funeral plans when he pushed himself out of the locker.

No one came for Dante. The outside world, as much as it had speculated and written article after article about it, would not entertain the idea as a real possibility. Something had simply been missed. Dead boys did not get up.

Except this one.

Half the population of Darkwood shared the skepticism. The others, the ones who had watched the story unfold from the start, had no room for doubt. Dante had been dead and nothing else. And now he was back.

Everyone at the church fell into the latter half.

They had been waiting for Jude the Sunday after Dante had risen. "Pastor, what does this mean?" One of them asked, the others echoing the same question.

"A miracle," Jude had answered. "Dante is blessed and was delivered back to us. He was meant to be here."

In the following weeks the proclamation raged over the town like fire. People, Dante's own neighbors, were suddenly asking him to grant his own blessings on them. "I can do no such thing," he tried to say.

"But you are holy," they countered.

They waited for him outside his house. They called him. They called his mother. Ceaseless, all hours, the crowd growing outside. For now, it was only a handful but how long until it was the whole neighborhood? The whole town? The state and then the country? The dreams never did stop. Always the same, that blaring horn ripping into the ends of the earth. The swarms of people amassed in the desert, skin scorching and peeling, all lined up for his mark.

When someone knelt to Dante in the middle of the grocery store, when he was out with his mother just trying to get dinner for the week, he had enough. That next Sunday, Dante went to church for the first time since he was killed.

Jude could set them straight, he thought. The man had to. Except when Dante stood with Jude at the podium, waiting for the denouncement before the dozens of beady eyes stalking him, Jude only frowned when Dante said he was not holy.

"Perhaps you are, though, Dante," Jude said. "It is up to every single person to accept the truth before them. That is the faith of it."

Dante stared at him slack-jawed, stricken. Jude, who knew better than anyone else exactly what he was. "But I am *not*," Dante gritted through his teeth, trembling, trying not to cry in front of everyone. The betrayal was worse than when Jude killed him, he realized, and Dante suddenly felt more alone up there than he did when Jude bashed his head in.

"You were dead," Jude said. "And then you rose. That is all we have seen. Everything else we can know only through God."

"May he enlighten you all then," Dante spat, before rushing off and down the hall, into Jude's office, where he closed himself in and waited at Jude's own desk.

An hour later, Jude stepped inside, the door shutting soft behind him.

"Why wouldn't you tell them?" Dante snapped.

Jude scoffed. "Because I'm worried. You may

be the Antichrist, but we're still in deep Texas. They would destroy you."

"You think they could kill me anymore than you already have?"

The look on Jude's face soured, finally slipping from the casual, calm expression he always wore in church. The bitterness made Dante smug, pleased at the rise. "I think it is best to let them think what they want to," Jude said.

"You're still ushering in the end times. Line them up outside for me to damn, why don't you."

"I'm serving you, Dante."

"You serve me because he wants you to serve me."

Jude inhaled deep, running his hand through his hair. "...I know." He gazed at Dante sitting in his own chair and looked like he might tell him to get off, except he stayed quiet.

You would have asked me to move before, Dante thought. *Before you killed me*. Dante settled deeper into the soft leather, like it had always been his.

A bible was splayed open on the desk, left from Dante reading while he waited for Jude to finish. Dante touched the page gingerly. "There are two beasts in the book. There is me, the first beast with the wound upon its head. So where is the second, who directs all people to worship it?"

His eyes flicked up to Jude, cold in their bitter stare, gripping Jude in place.

"What have you been telling them, Pastor? While I've left you alone to guide your people."

"You're accusing me now?" Dante waited for Jude to sit across from him, the place where Dante sat, where everyone who visited him did. Instead, the man remained standing. "I say exactly what I said today."

"What you said today was practically an endorsement." Dante looked down at the pages. His bitter expression had fallen into something else, softer. Jude thought he might start crying. "I can't keep doing this," Dante whispered. "It's going to happen, at this rate."

"What else will you do?"

Will? Dante wondered if that was even the right question. Was there something he could do? He had tried to ignore it and Jude killed him. He had come back and tried to lay low, tried to dismiss it, and the fever of his resurrection only grew. He could see it all now unfolding before him, too easy. He was only seventeen now, but it would be years more before he was meant to come into power, and that was plenty of time for his name to worm out of Darkwood, across the state, the country, more and more. In his dreams, that voice was only growing louder, more urgent. *Go to Jerusalem.*

Maybe even if he stayed here, perfectly still,

Jude would still drag him there in the end. He had already done the first part. Was there any way for them to resist? Dante wondered if he and Jude were not the most hopeless creatures to exist.

"I don't know," Dante answered.

When Dante asked if he could go over to his friend's house for the night, his mother said sure and didn't ask which friend.

She wasn't afraid of him, exactly. But since he had come back, she had been acting strange around him. Did not look him in the eyes. Did not stay too long in the same room with him. When he wanted to leave, she always said yes, no matter how often he asked. He had gone to Jude's so much since returning that he was spending more nights there than his own home.

As much as it stung, he supposed he couldn't blame her. She had seen his body, she told him when he came back. She had seen his head bashed in, the blackened, rotten blood. He had been dead. She had already been grieving when he found his way to their door with nothing more than that blistering scar.

Dante wondered if that's all she could see, looking at him. Her dead baby.

A backpack was slung over his shoulder. His mother sat at the kitchen table under a pale-yellow dining light, reading a magazine. A lukewarm glass of melted iced tea sat off to the side.

He couldn't explain entirely the sudden ache he had when looking at her, but it settled deep in him. How long had they been in this apartment together? How many times had he seen an image exactly like this? His mother sitting at the kitchen table. The quiet serenity of the apartment, modest but warm, a place that was imprinted with the life of them.

"Mom?" He said. She looked up from the magazine. "I love you."

"Oh, Dante," she sighed. He thought she would only say it back, but she rose instead, crossed over to the front door where he stood. Her long, cool arms wrapped around him and suddenly they were hugging, her thick black hair brushing his face. "I love you too, baby."

Dante grit his teeth. His eyes stung but he breathed in deep, willing himself to not cry.

She ran her hand through his hair, nails scraping gently over his scalp. "Are you okay?"

He nodded. "Yeah, mom. I'm okay. I just... I don't know. I love you."

She laughed. "I know you do, Dante. It's alright, baby. Are you sure you still want to go tonight?"

Dante pulled back, shrugged his bag higher up. "Yeah."

She stood at the doorway with her arms crossed, waiting. He would walk out of his apartment to head up the street and down the corner where Jude would be waiting in his car, parked by the trees, to pick him up and take him back to his own house. For now, he glanced at his mom one final time as he opened the door and stepped out into the night. She waved from the warm light of the apartment and Dante was overwhelmed from the sheer gratitude that she had seemed scared of his revival, that she didn't want to talk about it, that she had not called him holy or blessed or anything like that. Only *"you came back to me,"* on the first day, when she broke down crying at the sight of him.

Be good, Dante thought as the door shut, the faded brown paint sealing them apart from each other one last time.

He and Jude were up until two a.m., even though they had gone to bed at ten that night. They had fucked until they were tired, sweating, and then they lay besides each other and talked, and when they had steadied, one would roll into the other and they would have sex again, needy, desperate, all hands gripping the other with nails digging in, until they'd exhausted themselves and talked again.

Neither needed to say they did not want to sleep. It was simply understood, a shared impulse that ran through the both of them. Ever since Dante had risen, the dreams had become nonstop for Jude too, not only when Dante was near but every night now.

That voice haunted them both, violence and hellfire always in the back of their minds, floating around as they ate breakfast, as they showered.

It was always waiting for them, cloaking over as soon as they fell asleep. Jude was no longer in the room anymore but in the desert at Dante's side. He saw the mass of people, withering in the scorching heat of the sun. He saw the earth split in half. He saw bodies rising. He saw exactly how the world would die, the blare of a horn piercing through.

Eventually he would fall asleep and it would be back. For now, he was awake in the room, staring up at the dark blue ceiling with Dante resting on his chest, his arms over Dante's thin back. The window was left open and the humid air fell warm and sticky over them. Outside, the grass rustled in the wind, insects chirping and singing in gentle rhythm.

"Jude?" Dante asked.

"Hm?"

"You'd do anything for me?"

Jude smiled, the sight obscured in the dark. He squeezed Dante a little tighter. "Anything."

"Will you leave with me?"

"Yeah. I'll go anywhere with you."

Dante pushed himself up to rest on his elbows, his arms digging into Jude's chest and ribs. The man didn't mind, Dante too lithe to really hurt him and even then, he didn't care. Jude reached up to run his fingers up and down the smooth skin of Dante's shoulders. Dante looked down at him, just enough light from the stars outside to make out the soft lines of his face.

Why do you look so serious all the time? Jude wondered as he stared back at Dante, meeting his gaze. Even before this all happened, Dante had always been so solemn, quiet and contemplative. It made him seem older than he was. Jude wondered now if it was because Dante was truly something ancient.

"What if I wanted to stop existing?" Dante asked. "What if I wanted to take us away to somewhere no one could ever find us?"

Jude's smile slipped, his expression relaxed. He lifted his hands to cradle Dante's face delicately, like he could ruin it if he wasn't careful, like it was the most holy thing he had ever touched. "My answer's the same. I'm yours, Dante."

He leaned up and pressed his mouth to the center of Dante's forehead, right over the soft, raised flesh of his scar.

In the morning, they settled into the car and drove away. Jude locked up his house, the church, and put the keys under the doormat where his father could find them. The dishes had been washed and put away, the trash taken out, the food in the fridge tossed into the high grass of the backyard where the raccoons and possums could finish it off. His clothes had been left still hanging in the wardrobe, unneeded for this trip or any time past it. The lights had been turned off. The stove and microwave and TV had all been unplugged, left to grow cold and unused.

Everything of Dante's was still at his house, in his room, where his mother would be able to pack them up when she was ready. His clothes, his books, his games and his computer, the college acceptance letters he had stuffed in his desk, the order form for his yearbook that he would never pick up and sign with the rest of his class, his graduation robe still in its plastic bag. Only his backpack of clothes, the one he always took to Jude's house, was in the backseat of the car with them. His one other possession, a cell phone, had been left on the bedside table in Jude's room, battery life low. After all the calls he would miss that day from his mother, it would be drained and dead by nightfall.

They drove out of the town, and then out of the state, and then they kept driving. For hours, Jude took them through back roads and highways, into towering cities, across open fields with a single house speckled in a hill every few miles, Dante staring out the window the whole time.

They didn't know where they were going. All Dante knew was he wanted to drive farther and farther still, away from where they had been raised, away from anyone that had ever known them. If he could have named a place he was looking for, as they drove into the splitting light of the sun setting before them, bright golden and red lines cutting across the horizon of the road, Dante would have said they were heading to the edge of the world.

The day passed and then another, and then another, and then a week. They stopped at gas stations to get food, bags of sunflower seeds and honey buns, jerky, water bottles and coffee. They parked in the deep woods and the far off in the desert and slept together in the backseat, crawled over each other in the tight space to fuck when it was nightfall and the blue light of the moon washed over them.

As they drove deeper, with each mile crossed, each new town passed, the dreams became more muted. Every new night they heard the voice a little lower. The desert flashed before them in pieces and it was not scorching day but night there, and then bodies became quiet, and then it was only Jude and Dante together, passing barefoot through a cool stone temple with the voice so soft over them it sounded like only a song from somewhere far, far away.

He could feel the grip of it fading. The dreams, the end of times. Not only fading from him and Jude but the air around them, the entire sky a little lighter, a little sweeter. Dante was escaping more and more from the chance for anyone to ever bow to him. There would be no marks. There would be no angels coming down. There would be no great suffering. The horn would not come.

They were driving into the next state. It was high noon, sunlight painted all around them. Jude had put on the radio and Johnny Cash was playing. Dante's window was rolled down and the wind whipped over his hair, his feet up on the dashboard. He sipped coffee from a thin gas station paper cup, the plastic of the lid brittle. It was lukewarm by now, having bought it hours ago. Every now and then Jude asked him to hold out the bag of trail mix so he could grab some and Dante did.

The dreams from last night were barely there. Only flashes of images. A sound he had forgotten within a few minutes of waking.

Dante looked out the window to watch the passing transmission towers, stark against the blue sky like beacons, and wondered if Jesus wasn't actually the first child—if Jesus was the only son who did what he was supposed to, the first to turn away from temptation. He wondered if there wasn't another Antichrist before him, maybe several more, a long chain of his kind that all ended up too in awe of and in love with the world to hurt it. Too in love with the person next to them to let it happen.

THEY COULDN'T REMEMBER WHAT STATE THEY
were in or what town they just came from when
Dante told Jude to turn into an off-road.
Wilderness was all around them, jagged cliffs
cutting into the sky, a thick forest of trees
between the mountains and cloaking over. Jude
drove down an unpaved path that rattled the car
until it ended in a small area he thought was
meant to be a parking lot. They got out and
Dante left his bag in the car, his wallet. Jude did
the same.

Neither knew where exactly they were
heading but an innate sense passed through
them. Dante was pulled through the woods by
it, and Jude was pulled to Dante, following him.

They hiked through the land and cliffs for
hours when they came across the wide, dripping, blackened mouth of a cave. They were
tired when they found it, sore from the travel.
Still, Dante took Jude's hand and the two of
them went in.

Like the drive, Dante did not know exactly
what he was looking for. He only knew he
needed to go deeper, and then deeper still. They

walked for hours, only speckles of the broken surface of the cave allowing any sunlight to come through. Eventually the ground lowered and there was nothing but pitch-black. It was a darkness Dante had never seen before, so deep without the light pollution of the country, the small porch lights off in the distance, the street-lamps, the moon and the stars.

Dante wondered if he would run into the wall of the cave, or a jagged dome of sediment, but they never did. They should have at least run into something else living, and at any moment he thought he would step on a snake, hear a bat. But inside was just nothing except for the sounds of their breathing, their foot-steps, and the quiet sound of water dripping.

They walked for what Dante thought was hours, maybe halfway into the night, before Jude and him lay down on the cold floor of the cave. Jude let Dante fall asleep right on top of him, cushioned from the freezing stone on the warm skin and muscle of his body. There were no dreams.

When they woke, whatever time it was, the two of them stood up and kept walking further. The ground sloped low, the smell of the cave sharp and clean all at once, the air of it damp. They walked and they slept and they walked and slept until Dante's feet started to bleed inside of his shoes, the soles of them unraveling, his skin covered in broken blisters. When Dante could no longer take a step without falling, Jude leaned down to pick him up and carried him deeper still.

They were walking for so long that Dante started to think they weren't on Earth anymore. Like they had taken a certain turn and found a place removed from the rest of the world. *Maybe we are returning to Hell,* Dante thought, and marveled at how much colder it was than he had ever imagined, how calm and quiet it was. How intimate, curled in Jude's firm arms, cool air lapping at his raw feet, shoes long abandoned. Wherever they were, Dante rested easy in the thought that it was a place no other person could ever go. It was a place he and Jude could no longer escape, even if they wanted to, blind and lost in the dark of the pit.

Eventually the walls begin to close in on them. Some turn far back that Jude took led them there into narrowing walls, cave starting to scrape at his shoulders. Jude kept walking until the ceiling dragged across his hair, and then when he could no longer walk, he set Dante down and they hunched down more and more until they were crawling.

They clawed forward on their hands and knees for another hour more, until even that became too cramped. In the end they had cornered into the tunnel of sediment, Dante laying on top of Jude, the two of them crushed together between the rock and unable to go any further.

It had been days since they'd eaten, too long since they had water. Their muscles were wrought, bodies exhausted from the never-ending walking, the constant shivering from the merciless chill of the cave.

As they started to drift off, close to sleep again, Jude leaned up to press his mouth to Dante's forehead. There were no thorns upon his head for Jude to hurt himself on, Dante thought, but he imagined horns sprouted from his head all the same.

ACKNOWLEDGMENTS

Thank you to my family, including my mother, who taught me empathy for all living things despite my evil heart, and is no longer alive to see that I actually did keep up with the writing and did not get trapped down in Texas. You would have been deeply uncomfortable with this book, and you would have been proud of me anyways.

Thank you to my long-time best friend, Ashley, who has saved me time and time again, and was kind enough to read my rough draft and offer feedback. I love you so much. Huge appreciation to Franco, Julie, and my other early readers, whose feedback helped me navigate a kind of person I did not understand and helped refine my characters, and who assured me that the book was ready to make it out into the world.

Thank you to my New York friends, who has championed and supported my book since they heard about it. I never imagined it would have so many people awaiting its release.

Finally, thank you to the entire CLASH team for taking my book on, and to Christoph for giving me a chance; I'm so thrilled someone shares my love for the Antichrist. Forever grateful this strange story found its home.

ABOUT THE AUTHOR

M. Jane Worma is a queer horror writer with a fascination for the sadistic and horrifying. After escaping from their birthplace of San Antonio, Texas, and spending a decade in the haunted desert of New Mexico before making the move to the colder northeast, they now happily reside in Brooklyn.